Good Things Come on Tiny Wings: The Adventures of Petalwink the Fairy®

Presents from
Petalwink

by Angela Sage Larsen

To Isabel
10/2012
Love,
Grandma &
Papaw

For our Teachers:
Marilynn, Jack, Gordon & Ed

RISING STAR
STUDIOS
MINNEAPOLIS, MN

For other great resources contact Rising Star Education
888-900-4090
www.risingstareducation.com

Fairy Fest Gift List:
Felicia - Scarf
Francis - gourmet
        bugs
Twins - Fairyland
        Game
George Rabbit -
self help book
"Shrews & Bad
Moods: How to Tame"
June Bug - inkwell
Birdie - pearl
Gordo - surf leaf
Bliss Squiggle -
        new tie

days till
Fairy Fest:
0

Fancy MATCHES
ALL

First light broke over Newman Forest's
still-dozing brood,
but Petalwink the Fairy was awake
in an excited good mood.

The Forest Fairy Fest was
mere moments away,
and she was nearly ready for
everyone's favorite day.

Petalwink was proud she'd been so organized . . .
her presents all wrapped,
her generosity exercised.
She couldn't wait to see the looks
on all her friends' faces:
sweet smiles, some tears; their grateful embraces.
Petalwink yawned and stretched,
preening proudly for the day.
Then as she looked 'round her room,
she was filled with dismay!

Her nest had been ransacked
while she slept through the night;
her special gifts all missing, boxes empty—
a terrible sight!

Fairy Fest Gift List:
Felicia - scarf
Francis - gourmet
          bugs
Twins - Fairyland
          Game
George Rabbit -
self help book
"Shrews & Bad
Moods: How to Tame"
June Bug - inkwell
Birdie - pearl
Gordo - surfleaf
Bliss Squiggle -
          new tie

thanks
and
sorry.
-B

Her holiday felt ruined now
    because her friends would never know
    how thoughtful she was—
as her extravagant gifts would surely show.

She ignored the call to gather by old Rockstack Wall,
deciding instead to pout, bury her face, and curl up in a ball.

Missing her at the morning's event, Felicia came by
to bring her a gift (intruding on Petalwink's good cry).

Ignoring the pretty painting
Felicia had specially made,
Petalwink also refused to join
the Flying Fairy Parade.

When breakfast came and went
with no Petalwink,
Francis came to find her
and brought a warm drink.
A muttered "thanks"
was all the fairy could muster,
as she thought how this day
had lost all its luster.

After a rousing game of Dizzy Birch
   that she then missed,
the twins thought to cheer her
   with a round of Fairy Twist.
But Petalwink just pouted
   about the twist of fate
that robbed her of praise
   for giving presents so great.

Then George Rabbit came
    before nap time and quiet reflection.
Though grumpy as usual,
    his visit had his best intention.
He grumbled, "I don't care that you got me nothing,
    I got you the same."
(He might have liked his gift,
    the book *Shrews & Bad Moods: How to Tame*.)

June Bug wondered why her friend was a no-show;
   she knew Petalwink loved to dance in fresh snow.
Upon accepting June Bug's thoughtful gift sadly,
   Petalwink continued to act rudely and quite badly.

When all in the forest raised their voices in song,
Birdie Nuthatch noticed Petalwink didn't join along.
Missing her fairy friend touched her tender heartstrings,
so she visited, bringing hugs in her soft feathered wings.

Fairy Fest Gift List:
Felicia - Scarf
Francis - gourmet bugs
Twins - Fairyland Game
George Rabbit - self help book "Shrews & Bad Moods: How to Tame"
June Bug - inkwell
Birdie - pearl
Gordo - surf leaf
Bliss Squiggle - new tie

Gordo brought Petalwink
a savory Fairy Fest meal;
but even this late in the day,
he wasn't spared her sad spiel.

Before the last call
for the giving of thanks,
Bliss Squiggle slithered into her nest of pixie angst.
She moaned how she would not get glory in any way
for the presents she so carefully chose for this day.

Bliss said, "What counts is the thought
that you have for other folk;
you missed the joy of today by your own harsh stroke.
From within yourself can come the best gift;
then to your friends, your focus can shift."

Petalwink had mere moments to make a choice
    with the closing reception just underway,
    where all would rejoice.
She searched her nest, finding just piles of plain seeds
    as not much hope to supply any friends' needs.
But, as she started (at first very slowly) to think of each one,
    she realized her friends' beauty

                        and joy
                            and talents
                                and fun.

New offerings now in tow, she arrived just in time;
her gifts full of love . . . all without spending a dime.

She saw that Felicia
liked her new pretty vase;

Francis Frog
loved his mixing bowl—
she could
tell from
his face.

Willow & Whitney's Acornball Tourney would be a big hit . . .

George Rabbit's time-out spot gave him a place to sit.

June Bug's new paint pot
was pure inspiration;
and the fancy hat for Birdie,
a clever creation.
The hard helmet for Gordo
was just what he needed;
while the tie box for Bliss Squiggle
did not go unheeded.

Then they all
thanked Petalwink
for the nice gifts, of course.
But what they really liked
was the presents' sweet source.

"Never again," Petalwink vowed,
"Will ruining my own fun
with unthankfulness
be allowed."

Visit Petalwink.com to learn more about Petalwink and her friends, play games, sign up to be a Petalwink Pal by taking the Petalwink Pledge, and find out what Petalwink has been up to lately!

And . . . be on the lookout for *Petalwink Keeps a Promise*, the fifth storybook in the series, Good Things Come on Tiny Wings: The Adventures of Petalwink the Fairy®

Petalwink & You...

Sometimes nothing feels better
than a good think.
So take a moment now to think Petalwink!

🦋 At the beginning of the story, was Petalwink more excited about giving or about making herself look good?

🦋 Why did Petalwink miss out on all the celebrations on her favorite holiday?

🦋 What were some of the nice things her friends did for her to try to help her feel better?

🦋 What are some nice things you've done for someone else to make them feel better when they needed it?

🦋 What did Bliss Squiggle mean when he said that it's the thought that counts in giving a gift?

🦋 Why do you think the presents Petalwink gave her friends at the end of the story might have been even better than the first presents she was so proud of?

🦋 What does it mean to be generous?

www.Petalwink.com

Angela & Whit Larsen (with Daisy)
Author/Illustrator & Business Manager

Angela and Whit have been in business together since they got married. First, they owned and operated a studio and gallery in Healdsburg, California. Then, after Petalwink made her first appearance at the gallery and started telling her story, they moved to Whit's home state, Missouri, and formed a business called Three Trees, Inc. to get Petalwink's message out. They now live in O'Fallon with their yellow dog, Daisy, and work full-time on the Petalwink character education book series.

This is the fourth book in the series of seven. The series spreads Petalwink's message of giving, imagination, and believing in yourself and the greater good. Three Trees, Inc. often works with children's charities. To find out more about Petalwink and her friends, other books in the series, the Petalwink brand, and Angela & Whit, visit www.Petalwink.com